STARRING SPIDER-MAN

BY RICH THOMAS JR.

ILLUSTRATED BY
RON LIM AND LEE DUHIG

Los Angeles
New York

FEATURING YOUR FAVORITES!

kid from Queens

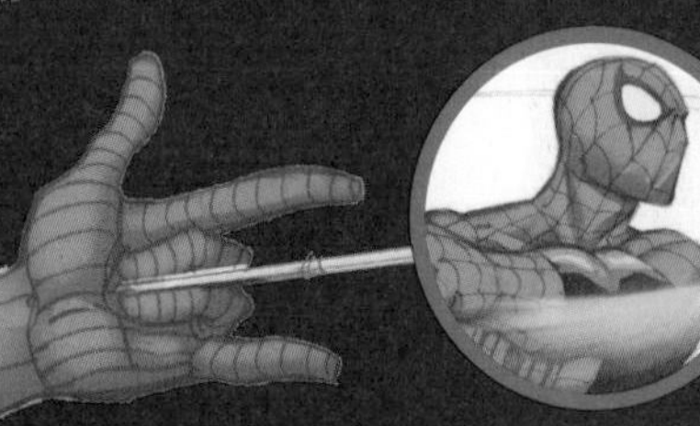

The Crush

SPIDER-MAN

PETER PARKER

Gwen's dad

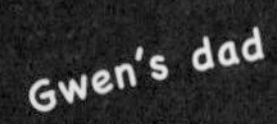

GWEN STACY

CAPTAIN STACY

NOVA

DAREDEVIL

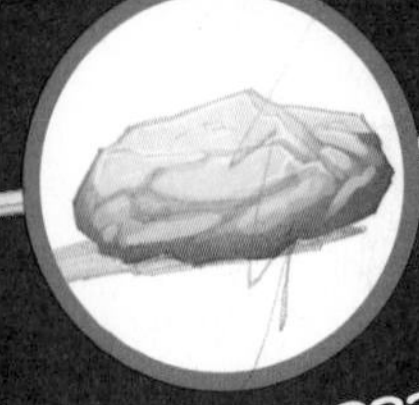

VIBRANIUM???

CAP'S SHIELD

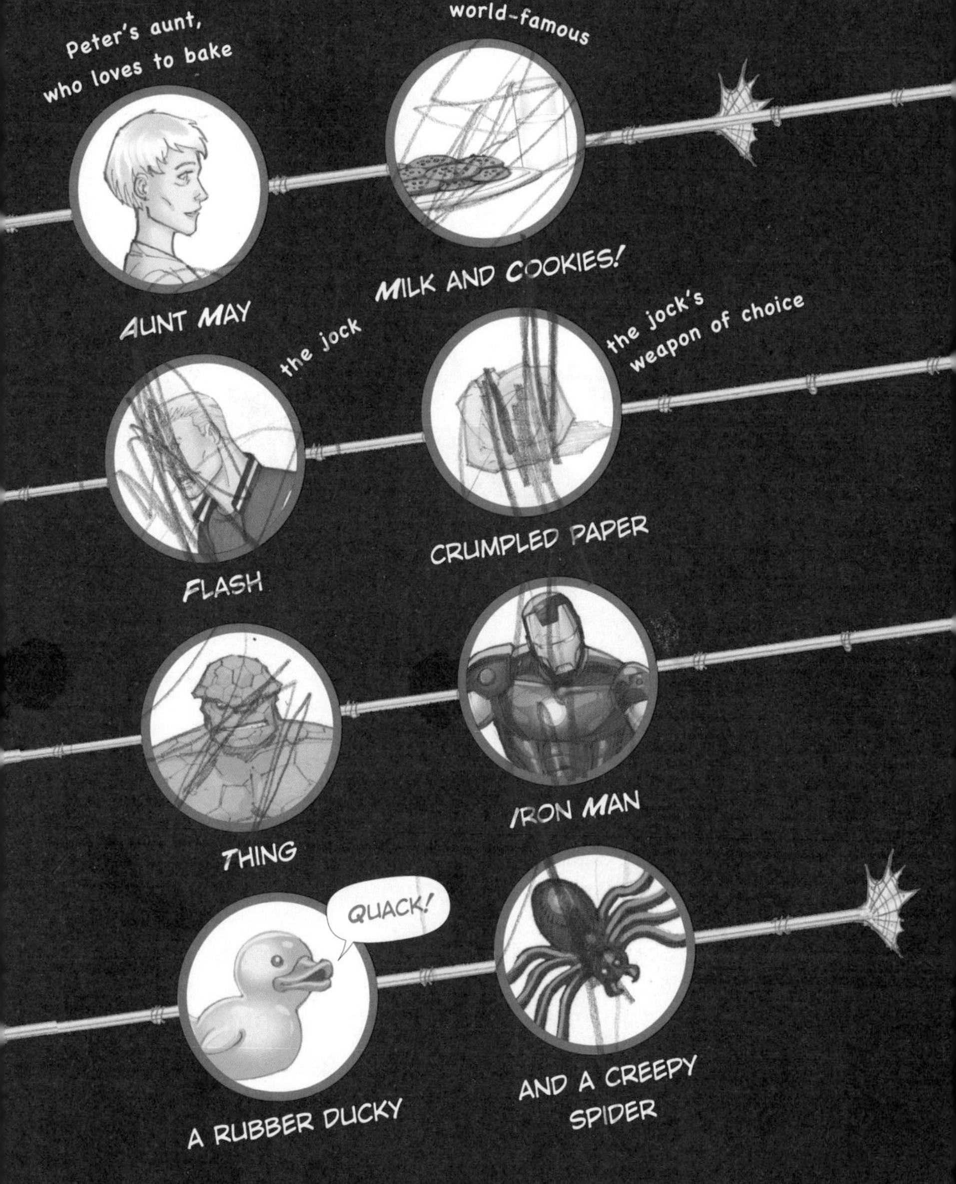

Peter's aunt, who loves to bake

AUNT MAY

world-famous

MILK AND COOKIES!

the jock

FLASH

the jock's weapon of choice

CRUMPLED PAPER

THING

IRON MAN

QUACK!

A RUBBER DUCKY

AND A CREEPY SPIDER

THE STORY OF SPIDER-MAN

Peter Parker was just an average kid who loved science. While attending a presentation about radiation, he was bitten by a radioactive spider. This bite gave Peter amazing abilities. He could cling to walls, leap like a spider, and sense danger.

Peter used his scientific knowledge to create sticky fluid and web-shooters. With these he could spin webs and swing from skyscraper to skyscraper high above the streets of New York City. He created a costume and called himself

One night, Peter's beloved uncle Ben was killed by a burglar—a burglar Spider-Man could have stopped earlier that night but had decided not to. Peter was devastated. But he remembered something Uncle Ben had always told him: **WITH GREAT POWER COMES GREAT RESPONSIBILITY.**

He would never again pass up an opportunity to help. From that day on, Peter used his powers to fight for justice and defend the public. He stopped everything from petty thieves to Super Villains.

Peter has had countless amazing adventures since becoming Spider-Man. This is just one of them. . . .

CHAPTER

"Don't look up, don't look up, don't look up," Peter Parker mumbled. He squinted and tried to will away what was coming toward him.

"Hey, bookworm!" Flash Thompson called out from the other end of the hall. Peter looked up from his locker. Flash was Midtown High's quarterback and was always followed by a group of other jocks and adoring cheerleaders.

"THINK FAST!" Flash said as he tossed a balled-up piece of loose-leaf paper at Peter.

It bounced off his forehead and into his locker.

"Real funny, Eugene," Peter said. He never called "Flash" by his nickname, because he knew the jock hated his *real* name. "Maybe if you used paper for something other than throwing, you'd actually graduate high school before you're a senior citizen," Peter quipped.

"And maybe if you spent less time studying

and more time **RELAXING,** you'd have better luck with the ladies," Flash said, motioning to the giggling cheerleaders several lockers away.

"Luck, huh? Glad that's something you think you have, because it's all you've got," Peter shot back.

Flash waved his hand in the air to dismiss Peter. But Peter could tell by the look in Flash's eye that his comment had stung.

"Come on, crew. Let's not waste any more time with this loser," Flash said. Then he and his fan club headed down the hall.

Peter picked up the crumpled paper from

the floor of his locker. He opened it. Even though he wasn't surprised at what he saw there, he had to admit that it still bothered him.

He tossed the paper into the recycling bin. Flash shot a look back at Peter over his shoulder. By his smile, Peter could tell that Flash had seen him open the paper and throw it away. And the worst part was that Flash seemed to be enjoying every second of it. If Peter thought he'd stuck it to Flash before with his comment about Flash's need for luck, it was Flash who had the last laugh—as usual.

Flash and Peter went their separate ways—Flash to the schoolyard and Peter to the school library. Maybe Flash was right. Maybe Peter *did* spend too much time studying and not enough having fun. After all, it was lunchtime, and the rest of his class was outside enjoying the beautiful late-fall weather. He was holed up in the stuffy school library, preparing for the next week's science test. And he was the only one in there.

Well, *almost* the only one.

"HEY, PETE!" Gwen Stacy said.

"SHHH!" the school librarian scolded.

"I thought I was the only one who spent my lunchtime studying," she whispered.

"Even a girl as smart as you has to be wrong sometimes," Peter said, and he thought he saw Gwen blush a little.

"Well, I couldn't ask for better company," she replied.

Then it was Peter's turn to squirm uncomfortably. He set his books down next to her and took a seat. If Flash could see him now! For once Peter was happy to be a bit of an outsider. In this case it meant he got to spend time alone with Gwen Stacy. There was no

SHHH

way any other kid in his class would be joining them. Who else would pass up the beautiful weather for a study session?

Then the library door creaked open, and Peter couldn't believe what he saw.

FLASH was on his way in. What could he be doing in a library? Smiling, he slowly walked over to where Peter and Gwen were sitting.

"Hey, bookworm, I noticed you **dropped** this," Flash said, and handed Peter the drawing he'd thrown out just a few minutes earlier. There it was in plain sight. And

HHHHHHHH!!!!

Gwen was staring at it, too. What would she think? Would she find it funny? Would she laugh at him?

Peter **ripped** the paper off the table and grabbed his books.

"I've got to go," he said, and pushed the chair back, maybe a little too hard.

"SHHHHHHH!!!"

the librarian said again.

"But I was just doing my good deed for the day!" Flash said sarcastically.

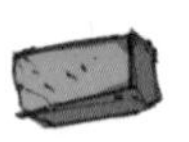

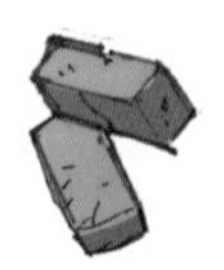

"You wouldn't know a good deed if it hit you like a ton of bricks!" Peter replied, imagining a ton of bricks falling onto Flash.

"How would you know about a ton of *anything*? You're such a weakling you couldn't even lift a *pound!*" Flash said.

Peter stormed out of the room and slammed the door behind him.

the librarian said so loudly that Peter could hear him through the closed door.

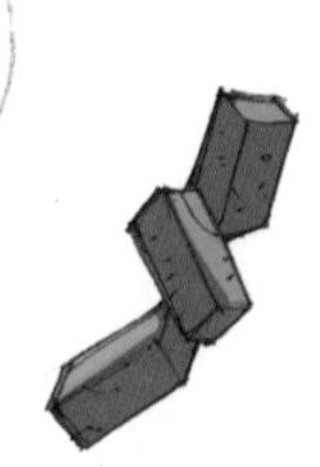

Peter was shaking.

He was *hurt*.

He was *embarrassed*.

But most of all he was **angry**!

CHAPTER

Peter spent the rest of the day distracted. In chemistry lab, his teacher noticed that he was not quite himself.

"Can anyone tell me the symbol for gold on the periodic table of elements?" the teacher asked.

When no one could answer, he turned to Peter, hoping his star student would know.

"Peter?" he asked.

"Huh? Oh . . ." Peter said. "Sorry, what were you asking?"

His teacher looked deflated.

"The symbol for gold. On the periodic table," the teacher repeated.

"UMMM, G???" Peter answered.

"**AU. AU** is the symbol for gold," the teacher said with disappointment.

And Peter was disappointed, too. He didn't like anyone getting the better of him. And Flash was certainly doing just that. He had him so down that Peter couldn't even concentrate in his favorite class. He couldn't even remember the most obvious answers.

But he did remember that piece of paper with the drawing and how he'd felt when Gwen saw it. Peter just wanted that day to end!

The bell **rang, rang, rang,** signaling the end of the school day. Peter made his way to his locker to collect his things.

"Pete!" someone called from behind him.

He turned to see Gwen.

"Hey, I just wanted to say that I think what Flash did before was a bit mean," she said.

"Yeah, well, I don't let it get to me," Peter replied, trying to smile.

"It sure doesn't look that way," Gwen said. "You're not your upbeat self. Don't let that jerk get to you. You'll be the one laughing when you've won a Nobel Prize and he's still repeating sophomore year."

Peter tried to imagine this.

"Thanks," he said, forcing a smile.

"You're welcome," she said, grinning. "Want

to go hang out at the Queensboro Coffee Shoppe? We can finish up our studying. Pick up where we left off in the library?"

Peter thought about it. It sure was tempting. But he knew he might not be the best company right now. He was in a really bad mood, after all. And besides, what if Flash busted in on them again? Peter was sure he wouldn't be able to hold back. And he couldn't hit Flash. Peter packed an unusually powerful **PUNCH.**

"I wish I could," Peter said. "But I promised Aunt May that I'd run a few errands before I got home."

Gwen looked disappointed, but understood. Peter searched for things to grab from his locker and paused, his eyes landing on his gym bag. Then, as Gwen walked away, he snatched it and made his way up to the school's top floor.

Peter looked around to make sure the coast was clear. Then he slipped into a small supply closet that he knew hadn't been used in years.

He unzipped his bag and took out his famous red and blue mask, gloves, and boots. He always wore the rest of his costume under his street clothes, just in case he needed a quick change. He put on the rest of his costume and relied on his special power—his spider-sense—to warn him if anyone was around.

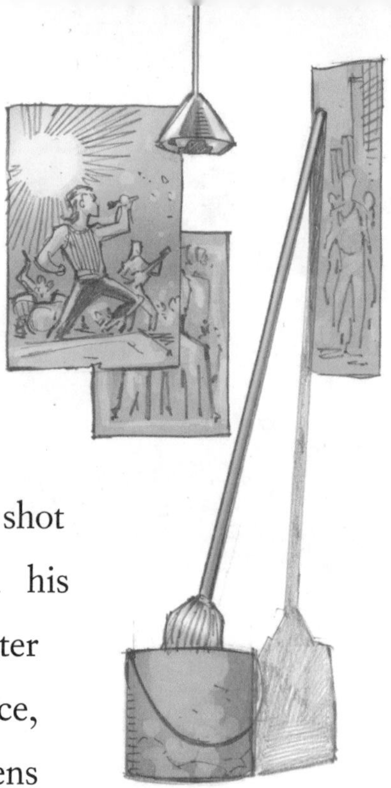

Confident, Peter sneaked up the stairs to the rooftop and pointed his wrists at the school's clock tower. Then he shot streams of webs from his web-shooters, and faster than anyone could notice, he swung out over Queens toward the city.

Being Spider-Man didn't mean Peter didn't have to deal with the same problems as ordinary teenagers. But it did give him unique ways of blowing off steam. One of his favorite ways was using his webbing to swing over the rooftops of New York and through the skyscraper canyons of Fifth Avenue.

Spider-Man swung his way to the Queens cable car that ran over the Queensboro Bridge into Manhattan. He shot his webbing at a car and hitched a ride under the cab into the city. The wall-crawler would make it to Manhattan in no time!

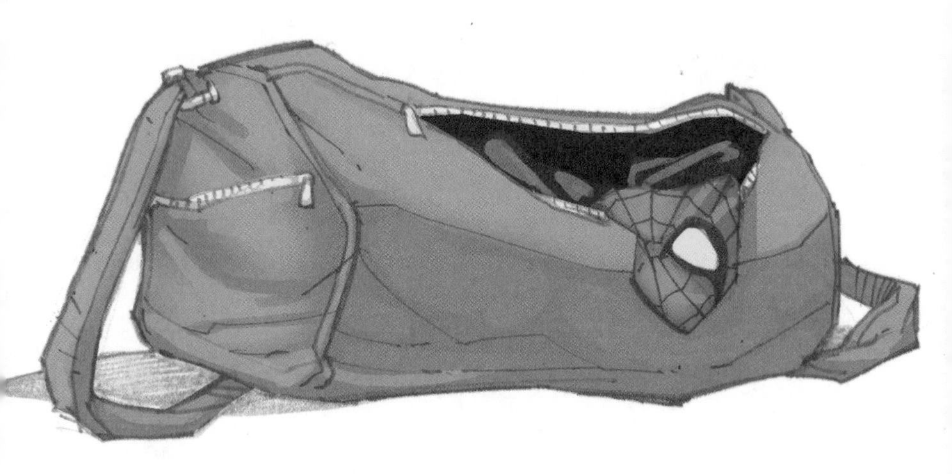

“Woo-hoo!!!!”

Peter hooted as he swung over the East River. There were few things that made him happier than this. He climbed up the side of the car and noticed a little boy looking out over the skyline with his hands against the window. Peter waved at the surprised kid, who smiled and waved back. The boy tugged on his dad’s

shirt, but before the man turned around, Peter was gone. He'd leaped off the cab and was swinging between skyscrapers and springing from water towers.

Soon he was in Central Park, swinging from the trees and enjoying the crisp fall air. He noticed people running and biking on the park trails, pointing up at him in amazement as he swung by. A little boy dropped his ice cream as he watched his favorite Super Hero swing right overhead. Everything was so different when he was dressed as Spider-Man. People were interested in him. They were excited when they saw him. They grabbed their smartphones and snapped pictures. It wasn't like school at all.

Peter looked down and saluted his fans. He loved the attention.

But being Spider-Man wasn't all about having fun. And Peter was reminded of this when his spider-sense began to *tingle*.

"Of course," Peter said. "Nothing like a problem to spoil a perfect afternoon."

As he continued to swing through Central Park, he looked for any sign of trouble. Then he noticed lights flashing from police cars. There were at least a dozen of them parked at odd angles in front of the

Museum of Natural History. Then he looked up and couldn't believe his eyes.

"What's going on?" he said.

Daredevil, another Super Hero, whom Spider-Man had worked with a bunch of times, was swinging away from the scene. Daredevil had a special extending billy club that he used to swing around the city the same way Spider-Man used his webs.

Daredevil turned around.

"SPIDER-MAN!" he said, looking at Peter.

Peter noticed Daredevil's glance. He must have been using his other senses to spot Spider-Man. After all, as Spidey knew, Daredevil was blind. No matter what had tipped him off, Daredevil started to flee over the city. Spider-Man chased after him. Both of the

heroes swung through alleyways, over rooftops, across bridges, and through tunnels until Spidey finally caught up with Daredevil to confront him.

"Hey, **DD,** what's up?" Spider-Man asked. He looked down. "Other than us, obviously."

Daredevil gritted his teeth and took a swing at Spider-Man with his billy club.

"Whoa. You in a bad mood or something?" Spider-Man asked.

Daredevil just grunted and swung at him again.

"Um, okay, if it's a fight you're looking for . . ." Spider-Man said, then lifted his wrists and shot webbing at Daredevil, and the pair began to struggle in midair!

In the clash, Spider-Man noticed something fall from Daredevil's belt. He shot a web to snatch whatever it

was. And in that moment of distraction he allowed Daredevil to escape.

Peter looked at the object he'd caught. It just looked like a chunk of metal—very heavy metal, but still metal. And if it came from the Museum of Natural History, it must be valuable. Peter rushed back to the gathered officers. He might have lost Daredevil, but he got something in return.

CHAPTER 3

"Here you go, Officer," Spider-Man said as he dropped the metal into the sergeant's hand.

"Wow, you Super Hero types never stop surprising me. One of you steals something, another one brings it back," the cop said.

"Honestly, I'm not sure what's going on. The guy who got away is usually on our side," Spider-Man replied.

"We know. Daredevil's helped us before, too," the sergeant said. "But he's now wanted for questioning."

None of this was making sense.

"Well, got to run—or SWING, I should say," Spider-Man said. "Hey, before I go, what's so special about that chunk of metal?"

"It's from the vibranium exhibit at the museum," the sergeant said. "It's the strongest metal on earth. Really rare. Captain America's shield is made from it. Better hope Cap doesn't go bad. This stuff would hurt if it was thrown at you!"

"Yikes!" Spider-Man said, not wanting to think about it. He waved to the officers, who thanked him; then he swung off across the river toward home. By the time he got there, the sun was setting. He swooped down behind his garage and changed out of his costume.

"Peter! I was worried about you!" Aunt May said when he finally walked into the house. "Where have you been?"

Aunt May had always been edgy. But she'd been worse since Uncle Ben died. She often thought the worst when Peter was running late. Peter kissed her on the cheek and smiled, which always made her smile, too.

"I'm sorry, Aunt May," Peter said. "I lost track of time studying after school, and then I got stuck on the train. I didn't have service in the tunnel, so I couldn't call."

Peter didn't like lying to Aunt May, but he couldn't ever tell her the truth. He couldn't tell her he was the amazing SPIDER-MAN.

"I'm just glad you're home," she said, squeezing his hand.

After dinner, Peter went up to his room to do his homework and was soon ready for bed. But he had a lot of trouble sleeping. He

wondered why Daredevil had stolen the vibranium. He worried about his upcoming science test.

Before he knew it, morning had arrived and it was time for school again. He wasn't sure how much he'd slept, or if he'd even slept at all. He felt like a robot going through the motions as he showered, brushed his teeth, and got ready for school.

"See you later, Aunt May," he said between yawns as he left the house.

"Peter!" his aunt called after him. "You forgot this," she said, standing at the door, holding his backpack. "You know, studying is great and important, but if you study too hard you'll just exhaust yourself."

Peter pecked her on the cheek and continued on to the subway, which he rode to school, completely wiped out from the night before.

“Hey, look who it is!” Flash shouted as Peter walked into Midtown High.

“Not in the mood,” Peter replied.

“Bookworm’s ‘not in the mood,’” Flash teased.

Peter opened his locker and yawned.

“Tired, Parker? What, was the Math-lete World Series on last night? Went into extra innings?” Flash said, elbowing his buddies for a laugh.

“Hey, check this out,” one of Flash’s friends said. “Somebody’s posted another angle.” He held up his smartphone, and there was a clip of Spider-Man battling Daredevil. Peter’s fight had gone viral!

“Ooooooh!!!!!”

"DUDE, LET ME SEE THAT," Flash said, grabbing the phone from his friend. "Man, he's freaking amazing. Send me this link. I want to print out some of those pictures and put them up in my locker. Maybe that's what I'll major in when I get to college—Super Hero. You can do that, right?"

Anytime anyone talked about Spider-Man around Peter, he became uncomfortable. He couldn't let anyone find out he was Spider-Man. So he never knew how to react.

"I don't think any of them go to college," Peter said. He was immediately sorry he said it.

"Huh?" Flash said.

"I don't think Super Heroes go to college. I think they're a bunch of dopes. I don't trust any of them," Peter said, not sure how to get out of the conversation without bringing more attention to himself and to Spider-Man. He felt himself blush a little at being put on the spot. Of course he didn't believe these things, but if the other guys thought he hated Super Heroes, they'd never discover he *was* one.

"HOHOHA!"

Flash laughed. "I think Petey here is scared of Spider-Man! Is that it? Is Petey-weety afwaid of spiders?" he said in a babyish voice, making "Itsy-Bitsy Spider" gestures with his hands.

Peter slapped his hands away.

"OUCH!" Flash shouted genuinely, grabbing one of his hands where Peter had hit him. Peter had held back his strength, but even a light tap from Spider-Man was going to sting a little. Still, Flash tried to make it look like he wasn't hurt.

As he walked away he shouted down the hall, "Better be careful, Petey. Spider-Man is going to get you! Bwahahaha!"

As Flash moved on to his class, Peter couldn't help burying his face in his locker and cracking a smile.

CHAPTER 4

On his way to his next class, Peter bumped into Gwen.

"Pete!" she said, smiling at him.

"Oh, hi, Gwen," Peter responded, smiling back.

"Hey, I just got an alert on my phone that says they have Wall Street blocked off. Some sort of thing going on at the stock exchange," Gwen said, looking concerned.

"My dad works down there," she continued. "I hope he's okay. I texted him but haven't heard back yet." Gwen's father was a captain in the New York City Police Department.

Peter's first thought was that he'd throw on his Spider-Man costume and swing down to the stock exchange to see what was up. He had actually almost moved to jump away from Gwen and up to the roof. Whenever he heard about trouble, his first thought was always to run off and check it out, and then help if he could.

But he stopped himself this time. He was there at school to learn. He couldn't run off every time he heard something *might* be wrong.

“Did they say what was going on?” Peter asked.

“Nope,” Gwen answered. “Just some news that blocks were roped off in the area.”

Peter decided to wait until he had more information. After all, the city was protected by one of the world’s top police forces. They could easily solve most of the city’s problems. And if it seemed like they could use a hand, he’d be there as fast as possible.

“Well, let me know what’s up,” Peter said.

"I'm sure everything's fine. You'll hear back from your dad soon. He's just got to be busy with everything that's going on down there."

"I hope so," Gwen replied.

For the next two hours, Peter couldn't keep himself focused on his schoolwork. He stared out windows, looking for police helicopters or other Super Heroes rushing toward downtown Manhattan. He fought the urge to go check out the scene. It was in his nature.

Then, just before the dismissal bell rang, Peter heard two kids in his English class whispering about the scene downtown.

If there was any truth to that at all, Peter had to get involved.

Brrrrrrinnnng Brrrrrrinnnng

Right after the bell rang Peter headed into Manhattan. He sneaked off the school grounds without anyone seeing him and swung quickly under the tracks of the elevated number 7 subway line on his way to downtown.

Before him was the New York Stock Exchange, and standing on top of it was his fellow Super Hero—and his good friend—Nova!

I don't care what anybody says. The subway is the quickest way to get around town.

Woo-hoo!
Transferring trains is a lot easier than it used to be.

CHAPTER 5

Okay, now I know something's up, Spider-Man thought.

He didn't know Daredevil all that wel
Sure, he knew enough to say that he was o
of the good guys. But he couldn't say
was totally, 100 percent, absolutely sure he'
never go over to the other side and become a Super Villain. But Spider-Man had fought beside Nova a bunch of times, and the two heroes had become pretty good friends.

Spider-Man shouted as he swung by. "Not sure what's going on here, but I'm sure it's all a great big misunderstanding. . . ."

"Spider-Man!" Nova said. He even *sounded* like a villain.

"Yeah, it's me, Spider-Man, your fellow Super *Hero*, buddy."

Nova lifted his hand and shot a blast at Spider-Man.

"Um, are you mad at me or something? If it has to do with that five bucks I didn't lend you for a sports drink a few weeks ago, I swear, I really didn't have it on me. . . . Yikes!" Spider-Man jumped out of the way as Nova sent another blast in his direction.

Meanwhile, Spider-Man's *spider-sense* was tingling like crazy. He looked down and saw that the police were trained on him as well. It looked like the entire police force was gathered below. There were sirens blaring and lights flashing all over.

“Surrender?” Spider-Man said.

“I figured you, or some other costumed creep, would try to stop me,” said Nova. “So I already warned the cops. I told them to expect other Super Heroes to arrive.”

“They think we’re working together?” Spider-Man asked, shocked.

Nova smiled. "Yep, exactly as I set it up. Worked like a charm. So, what do you say, Spidey? They already think you're a criminal. Why not reap the benefits and work with me here?" Nova asked.

"Have you lost your mind? Oh, sorry, obvious question," Spider-Man replied. "You clearly *have*."

"Come on, Spidey, if you can't beat me, then join me," Nova replied.

"No way, no how, pal. I have no idea what's gotten into you, or Daredevil, but I'm going to figure it out," Spider-Man said.

"Spider-Man and Nova, we are giving you another **SIXTY SECONDS** to surrender. We're prepared to act if you won't come peacefully," Captain Stacy announced.

"They're going to get you one way or another," Nova said. "If you try to run, they'll think you're in this with me anyway. Or you can help me and actually get something out of it."

"What do you want here, anyway?" Spider-Man asked.

"THIRTY SECONDS!"

Captain Stacy shouted.

"Will you help me?" Nova said.

"It depends," Spider-Man replied. "What do I have to do?"

Nova smiled. "The building has been evacuated. Through the third-floor window on the northeast corner, you'll see a notebook computer. It will help us hack into any financial

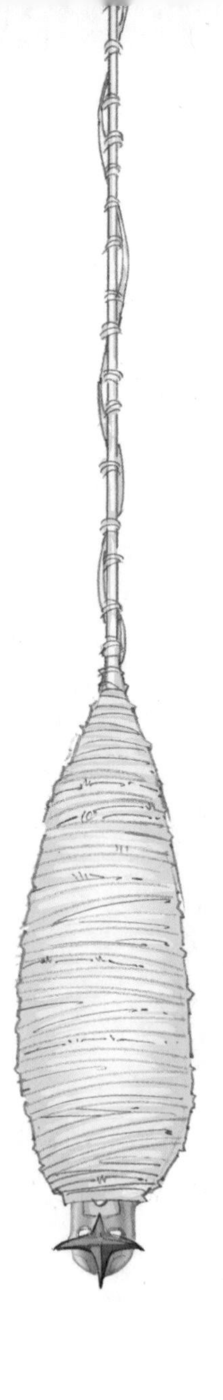

system in the world. We can divert funds. Grab it and I'll split whatever I snag with you."

"So that's what you're up to!" Spider-Man said, proud of himself for tricking Nova into telling him. "Thanks for the tip!"

"FIFTEEN SECONDS!"

Spider-Man swooped around behind Nova and fired his webs at him, turning him into a Super Hero cocoon! Nova was fastened tightly to the roof, and Spider-Man was getting ready to move in for questioning when he heard Captain Stacy yell from below:

"TIME'S UP!!!"

Before Spider-Man could do anything else, rockets filled with some sort of gas started to streak around him. He began to cough but was able to dodge the pellets with his super skills. He weaved his way around their paths and swooped into the third-floor window Nova had mentioned. He webbed the notebook and grabbed it, shoving it under his arm, and swung back outside.

The cops were still firing their gas, so Spider-Man took a deep breath and swung down over their heads, avoiding it. He dropped the notebook to Captain Stacy.

"That's what he was looking for!"

Spider-Man shouted down to them as they continued to try to stop him. "Keep it safe!"

Captain Stacy looked up at Spider-Man skeptically. Peter nodded as if to say "Honest, Captain!" Captain Stacy looked down at the laptop.

Maybe Spider-Man is on our side, Captain Stacy thought.

Spider-Man saluted the cops, then shot a web at the flagpole on top of Federal Hall across the street and swung away. He took a quick look back at the stock exchange and saw Nova streak up into the sky and out of sight.

He must have slipped away while the cops were focused on me! Peter said to himself. Zero for two—first Daredevil gets away, now Nova. You're not doing too well here, Spidey.

Just when Peter thought he was clear, he heard police choppers overhead.

You have to hand it to those guys—they don't give up easily! he thought.

The copters swiveled and swerved to keep

track of him. But like an acrobat he tumbled and darted all over the city streets. When he was sure he was out of the copters' views, he slipped into an alleyway. He couldn't walk back out in his costume. But he didn't have anything to change into.

Spidey frantically took off his mask and made his way out of the alley, walking proudly in a suit of webbed-together garbage bags and a newspaper fedora.

He started walking down the street, hardly noticing the sideways glances he was getting. After all, to a guy who spends a lot of time swinging around the city in a red-and-blue suit, walking around in garbage bags was no sweat at all.

Two businessmen walked by and gave Peter a strange look. Peter tipped his hat to them and walked on. But he could still hear their conversation.

"*MAN, PEOPLE ARE GETTING WEIRDER AND WEIRDER IN THIS CITY.* Did you hear what's going on down at the stock exchange?" one of the businessmen asked his friend.

"Yeah, and now they're saying Spider-Man's involved, too," the other replied. "I never trusted those guys anyway. You ask me, they're too dangerous to be out there."

Peter shook his head. Two heroes—Nova and Daredevil—had gone bad, Spider-Man looked like a villain, a bully was bothering him at school, and the girl he was crushing on *might* be interested in him! Not to mention that he now had to ride the subway home wearing garbage bags and newspapers. How could things get any crazier?

And then Peter remembered: he had a science test coming up at the end of the week.

CHAPTER 6

Peter spent the next morning listening to Aunt May worry about Super Heroes in general and Spider-Man in particular.

"That Spider-Man really gets to me. I mean, why wear a mask if you don't have something to hide?" she asked.

Peter nearly smiled. Of course he wore his mask as Spider-Man in part so his enemies wouldn't harm the people he loved—to protect Aunt May—and here she was thinking he wore it to hide deep dark secrets about his intentions.

If she only knew . . .

When he got to school about an hour later, he found the usual mixed bag of talk: sports, music, celebrities, fellow students, and, of course, Spider-Man.

"DID YOU SEE THOSE CLIPS OF THE STOCK EXCHANGE?" Flash was asking one of his pals.

Peter rolled his eyes. Why did his locker have to be right next to Flash's?

"Man, not sure how Spider-Man does it, but he nails every crook in town."

Without thinking Peter jumped to his friend Nova's defense.

"NOVA'S NOT A CROOK,"

Peter fired back.

Flash turned around slowly.

"Figures he'd root for the villain," Flash said, right in Peter's face.

"What are you reading? The *Daily Bugle* Web site? Every other paper thinks Spider-Man saved the day," Flash stated.

"And I hate to do this, but I have to side with Flash here, Pete."

Peter turned around to see Gwen.

"My dad said himself that Spider-Man was a big help, even though he didn't give me details when I asked," she added.

"All I'm saying is I don't trust him, that's all," Peter said.

"And all I'm saying is you're just scared of

a *real* man like Spider-Man," Flash teased. "Afraid of what he'd do to a wimp like you? Huh?"

"FLASH, CUT IT OUT,"

Gwen said.

"Oh, sorry," Flash said as he threw his hands up. "Forgot you two geeks are in *love*."

"We're not . . ." Peter and Gwen said at the same time.

Flash biffed Peter on the head.

"Good choice, Parker. Her dad's a police officer. Maybe he can protect you from big, bad Spider-Man!" Flash said. "I'd watch my back when I'm walking to the subway if I were you. Look behind the shower curtain when you walk into the bathroom. Check under

your bed before you go to sleep. Spider-Man's coming for you. . . ." Flash said in a singsong voice.

"Ignore it, ignore it," Peter whispered.

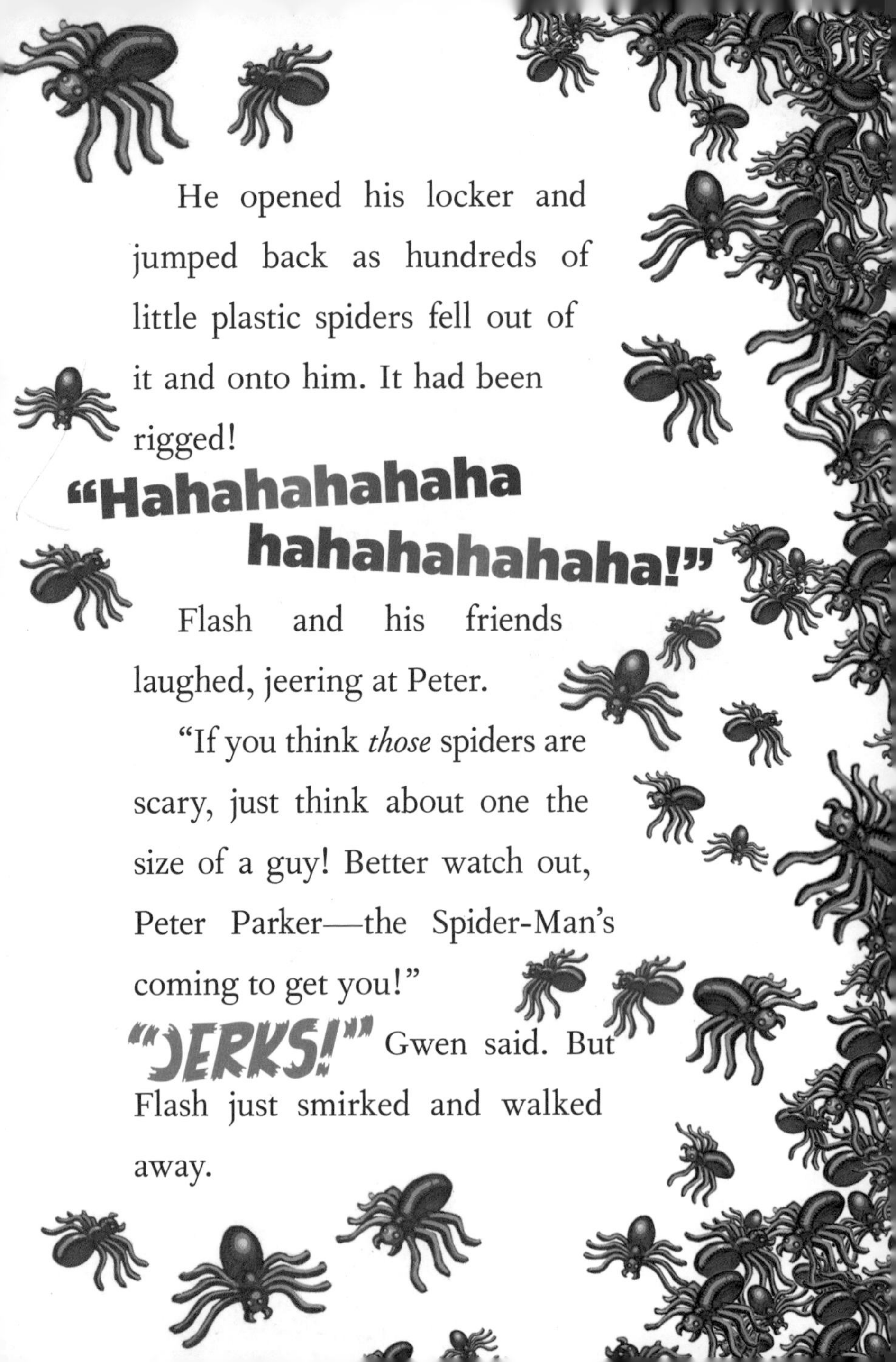

He opened his locker and jumped back as hundreds of little plastic spiders fell out of it and onto him. It had been rigged!

"Hahahahahaha hahahahahahaha!"

Flash and his friends laughed, jeering at Peter.

"If you think *those* spiders are scary, just think about one the size of a guy! Better watch out, Peter Parker—the Spider-Man's coming to get you!"

"JERKS!" Gwen said. But Flash just smirked and walked away.

Gwen grabbed a few toy spiders. "Here, I'll help you clean these up," she said to Peter.

"Thanks," he said. "You know, I didn't really mean you weren't . . . that I wasn't . . . I mean, when Flash said that thing about me and you, I didn't want you to think . . ." Peter stuttered, scrambling for the right words.

"Oh, I know, don't worry about it. Neither did I. I mean, neither do I. Oh, never mind," Gwen said, brushing her hair behind an ear nervously. "Um, I'll see you in chemistry, yeah?"

"Er, yeah. See you in a bit," Peter said. He could feel his face getting all **warm**. It was a stranger feeling than anything else he'd ever felt.

It was even odder than his spider-sense.

CHAPTER 7

That night Peter decided he had to put everything else out of his mind and study. He knew high school was important if he wanted to have any shot at a good college and a career as a scientist. He powered on his tablet and started to read about chemistry, from things as simple as water's molecular structure to things as exciting as unbreakable metal alloys.

Peter had forgotten how much he loved

science. He had been so distracted by other things recently. He had totally lost sight of one of the things that made him happiest.

As he read and researched, he quickly dismissed the dozens of app updates and push notifications that popped up on his screen—everything from weather alerts to newly available game levels.

But one notice he dismissed too quickly. He was getting tired. He'd been studying for hours. He was sure he must have read it wrong. Because he could have sworn he had read something that couldn't be true.

Did that say what I thought it said? Peter wondered.

He tapped his search engine app and typed in *News for Spider-Man*.

DAILY BUGLE

NEWS ALERT!

SPIDER-MAN HELD BY THING OF FANTASTIC FOUR

By Tomas Palacios and Clarissa Wong
Reports of heroes turning bad have come in from all over the city. First it was Daredevil attacking Spider-Man at the Museum of Natural History. Then there was the "Human Rocket," Nova. Now it's the Fantastic Four's very own Thing, who released an online video confessing his plans to terrorize the five boroughs. In the video, Spider-Man could be seen tied to a chair, being held captive by the bulky brawler.

SPIDER-MAN CAUGHT IN HERO'S WEB

By Jennifer Redding
What's happened to Spidey? That's the question on everyone's mind. . . .

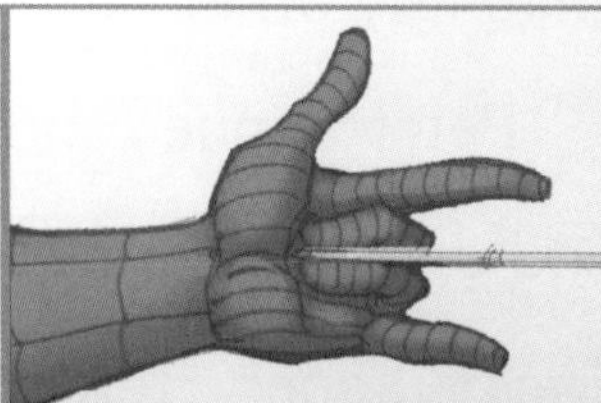

WHICH HERO IS NEXT TO TURN TO THE DARK SIDE?

By Ron Lim
Captain America? Thor? Wolverine? These are some of the names being thrown around the Internet these days. . . .

Peter chose the *Daily Bugle*'s Web site. He knew that the publisher, a man named J. Jonah Jameson, hated Spider-Man. Jameson was convinced the hero was a menace, as he called him. And he spent most of his time trying to get the public to believe Spider-Man was a villain, too. But Jameson also had the best reporters in the business. So even though he forced his staff to paint Spider-Man in a bad light, the stories usually had more information than any other news source.

Peter tapped on a link to a video. He couldn't believe what he was seeing! The big, rocky Super Hero known as the Thing was standing in a dark room with what looked like Spider-Man tied to a chair in front of him.

"WHAT THE HECK?" Peter said.

Peter pressed play. The clip began to run.

"IF YA HAVEN'T NOTICED, A BUNCH OF US ARE TIRED OF PLAYING THE PART OF THE SUPER HERO. WE WORK NIGHT AN' DAY PROTECTING YOU PEOPLE, AND WE GET NOTHING OUT OF IT," the Thing said. "SO WE'RE GONNA TAKE WHAT YOU OWE US, WITHOUT ASKING. CONSIDER IT PAYBACK. DAREDEVIL IS ON BOARD WITH US, AND SO IS NOVA. AND EVERY DAY MORE AN' MORE STEP FORWARD. THEY WANT TO JOIN THE SUPER HERO RESISTANCE.

"BUT THIS BOZO OVER HERE HASN'T DONE ANYTHING BUT GET IN OUR WAY."

"AND BECAUSE OF THAT," the Thing

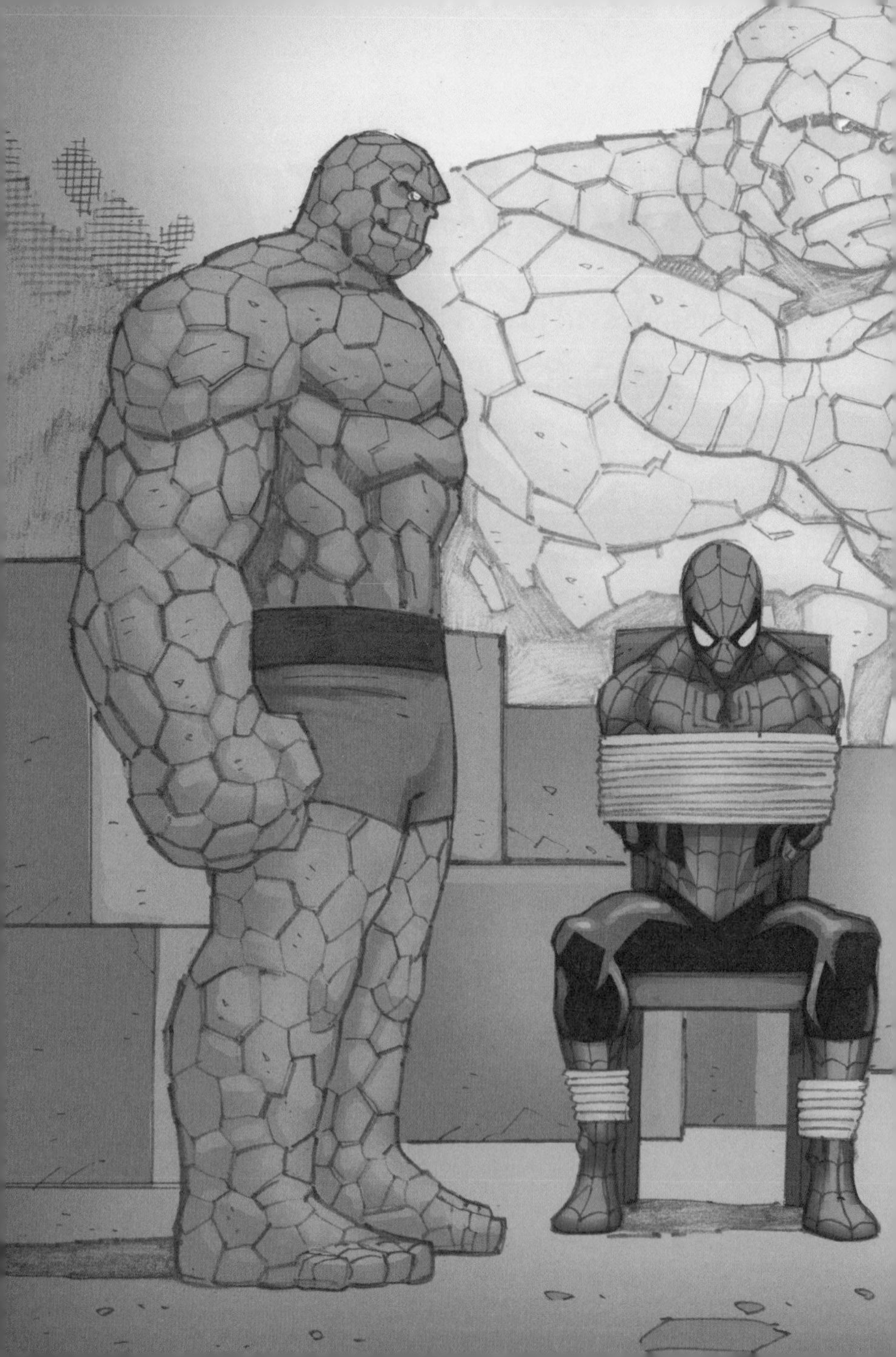

continued, as he SLAPPED his captive Spider-Man upside the head.

Whoa! Peter flinched. Even a love tap from the Thing would hurt! he thought.

The Thing went on. "WE'RE GOING TO *MAKE* HIM HELP US. IN FACT, WE'RE GONNA KEEP HIM LOCKED UP IN HERE TO DO OUR DIRTY WORK. **OUR REAL DIRTY WORK**, THAT IS—CLEANING THE TOILETS, IRONING OUR COSTUMES, WHATEVER."

It was weird for Peter to see himself on-screen in that position, even though he knew the guy on the screen wasn't *really* Spider-Man.

"SEE, YOU GOT TWENTY-FOUR HOURS. IF YOU HAND OVER THE LAPTOP THIS GUY OVER HERE SNAGGED FROM US, WE'LL SET SPIDER-MAN FREE. OTHERWISE, WE SQUASH HIM LIKE THE

BUG HE IS, AND ME AND NOVA AND DAREDEVIL AND A WHOLE BUNCH OF OTHER HEROES DESTROY THE CITY, ONE BOROUGH AT A TIME. AND WE TAKE THE SPOILS FOR OURSELVES.

"AND JUST IN CASE YOU PEOPLE DON'T CARE IF SPIDER-MAN LIVES OR DIES, I HAVE A SPECIAL TREAT FOR YOU. I'M GONNA UNMASK THIS GUY. EVEN IF SPIDER-MAN DOESN'T HAVE ANY FRIENDS OR FAMILY, THE GUY UNDER THE MASK PROBABLY DOES. THAT MEANS SOMEONE'S BOUND TO STEP UP."

Peter leaned in. This was getting weirder and weirder.

The Thing's big rocky hand clenched the mask of the Spider-Man on the screen. The Thing whipped it off and revealed the wall-crawler's true identity. **Spider-Man was really . . .**

FLASH THOMPSON?

CHAPTER

"Whoa," was all Peter could utter.

He stared at the screen. How in the world had Flash Thompson wound up in this situation? And where had he gotten that cheesy Spidey suit? I mean, mine looks waaay better

than that, Peter thought. None of this was making sense. Was it all just a trap? Was Flash in on it?

Someone knocked on Peter's bedroom door.

"Come in," Peter said, and Aunt May entered.

"Peter, there was just a report on the TV," she said, sounding very nervous. "A boy from your school's been kidnapped. A boy named **EUGENE**. They're saying he might be Spider-Man!"

"I know, I saw," Peter said.

"Well, please, *please* be careful, Peter. Shut and lock that window," she said while shutting and locking it herself. "These Super Heroes can **fly**, they can blast through walls—sometimes it seems there's nothing they can't do."

"In that case I'm not sure how much a locked window's going to do," Peter chuckled.

She took his hand. "I couldn't bear if something were to happen to you."

Peter kissed her on the cheek.

"I CAN TAKE CARE OF MYSELF," he said. And although Aunt May smiled and nodded, Peter could tell by the look on her face that she didn't believe him.

"I've got some homework to finish up," he sighed. "Don't worry about it, Aunt May. We'll be all right. Who's going to come looking for a random lady and her nephew in the middle of Queens? I mean, what would they get out of it? Unless they're looking for your chocolate chip cookies. I can see that, actually. They're worthy of an attack on the house!"

This managed to get a chuckle from Aunt May, who closed the door as she left the room, wishing Peter luck in his studies.

But Peter wasn't laughing at all, and he definitely wasn't thinking about his studies. As soon as he was alone, he started to research more about the story. According to what he read, no one knew where the clip had been

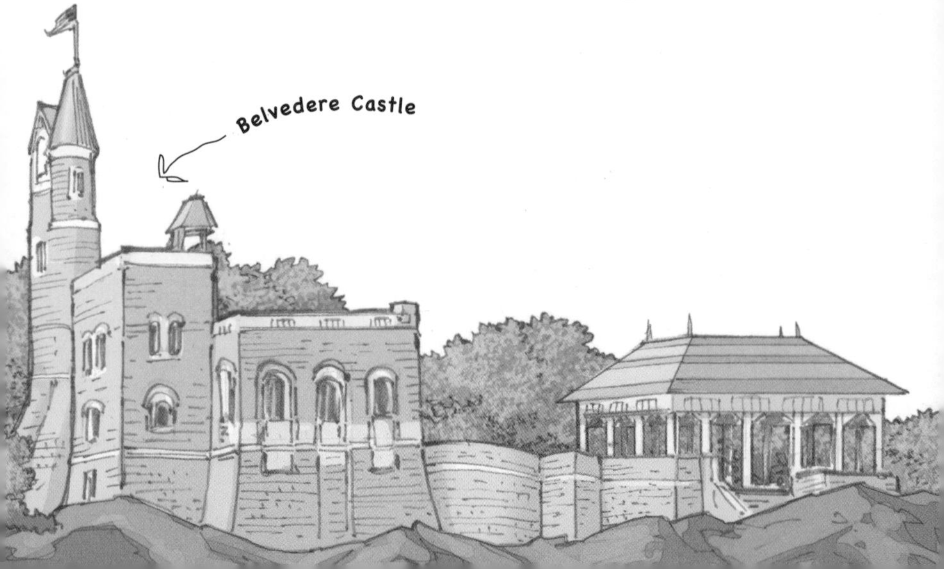

filmed. The DAILY BUGLE site said that the Thing had contacted it saying he and the other fallen Super Heroes wanted the laptop dropped off at Belvedere Castle in Central Park. Police had already roped off and searched that area and found no sign of the Thing, Spider-Man, or anyone else.

Peter paused. It didn't *really* sound like Flash's life was in danger. The Thing had basically said they were going to turn Flash into their housekeeper. He'd have a miserable life. He'd spend every minute worried that the heroes were waiting around every corner, ready to toss orders at him. He'd be afraid to simply walk down a hall. Basically, he'd feel the same way he made Peter feel every day at school.

Maybe Spider-Man didn't need to get involved in this one. After all, it looked like the cops had it under control.

And if they didn't, wouldn't Flash just be getting what he deserved?

Peter turned off his tablet, lay down on his bed, and stared at the ceiling. He was imagining his new, easy life at school without Flash.

He thought about it a lot.

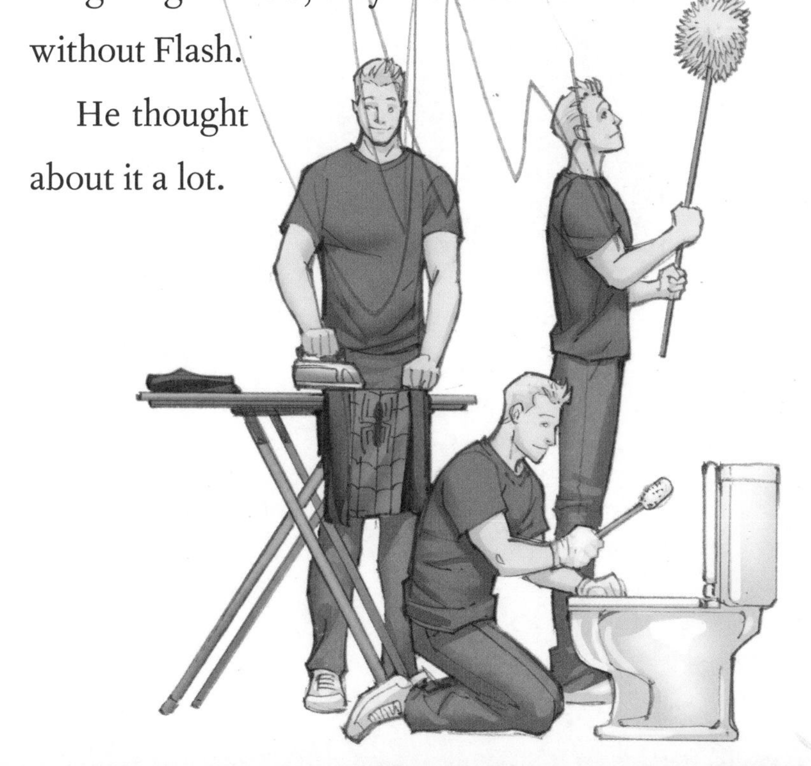

And after a long while of thinking about it, when Aunt May was asleep and the house was quiet, Peter put on his Spider-Man costume. He leaped from his window and swung toward New York City. As much as Peter disliked Flash Thompson, Spider-Man needed to save the day.

CHAPTER

In no time, Spider-Man had swung over the bridge and straight to Central Park. He carried an old, broken laptop tucked away in his costume. He'd dug it out of his closet and stripped it, knowing he could always use the spare parts for his tech experiments. Then he had taken the shell of the machine with him to Central Park.

He saw Belvedere Castle in the distance. It

was a huge building made to look like a grand palace. It overlooked a quiet pond and sat next to the park's Great Lawn. Best of all, it was surrounded by trees. This made it easy for Spider-Man to sneak past the police. He climbed into the treetops and made a web tightrope from one to another, walking over the heads of officers who were guarding the castle. When he reached a group

of trees that overlooked the palace, he shot a web toward its tower and swung down to the courtyard where the *Bugle*'s article said the Thing wanted the laptop left. Right after Spider-Man dropped it off, he swung back up into the trees, completely unseen.

Then he waited in the trees.

NOTHING.

Spider-Man had hoped that whoever was behind this had been watching the castle. He thought they'd show themselves when he dropped the laptop off, but no luck. The police barricade must have kept the place clear. Spider-Man needed to move to Plan B. He took out his phone and zoomed in on the castle courtyard and the computer and began recording.

"I've delivered the laptop, as you've requested. Now, set Spider-Man free," he said in a voice much deeper than his own. Then he created a fake name, uploaded the video to VidTube, and sent an e-mail to every media outlet he could think of.

In just a matter of minutes, he noticed the police starting to move in. But before they even got close to the castle, Spider-Man heard a roar overhead. He looked up and saw something shooting across the sky. It sounded like a jet's roar, but it was moving way too fast.

The streak shot down to the courtyard, near where the laptop was, and then darted right back up into the sky. Spider-Man knew he was about to lose the laptop and whoever had taken it. Worse still, he had a feeling that they weren't going to keep up their part of the deal and return Flash Thompson.

Spider-Man needed to act, and fast. As the streak of red and gold whizzed overhead, Spidey shot a web at the heels of the flying figure and was soon jerked up. He was whisked away, over the park and New York City, riding behind the criminal like a windsurfer. He held on tightly to the webs as he soared over the skyline at what felt like light speed.

He guessed that whoever he was following hadn't felt the webs attach to him and had no idea Spider-Man had hitched a ride. Skyscrapers and bridges seemed to zoom by. The water below was calm, but surely cold this time of year. As they started to descend, Spider-Man worried they were going to land right in it.

But upon hitting the ground, he discovered they'd landed on one of the many small islands that surrounded the city—the ones that were off limits to almost everyone and hardly ever occupied.

Spider-Man looked up, and looking directly back at him was

"You've gone bad, too, huh?" Spider-Man said.

He expected Iron Man to raise up his hands and blast him with one of his repulsor beams. But he just tried to run—and in a pretty clunky way, at that.

"Um, you're not actually Iron Man, are you?" Spider-Man said to whomever was limping away from him. One thing was sure—the guy trying to pass for Iron Man wasn't doing such a great job of it.

Spider-Man shot his webs at the fleeing suspect. The bad guy quickly got tangled up and fell down. Spidey ran up to him and noticed that he was wearing a good—but not nearly perfect—replica of one of Iron Man's suits of armor. He tore off the man's helmet and gasped. He was face-to-face with a hairless man whose pale skin was so white he could practically see his veins beneath.

"Where's Flash?" Spider-Man asked.

The villain laughed, as if to say he wasn't going to tell him.

Spider-Man looked around. The island was very small. It could fit no more than a few houses on it. He spotted a crude shack on the opposite shore. He rushed there and tore off the splintered door.

And there he was: Flash Thompson. He was tied to a chair, still wearing the Spider-Man costume without his mask. And he looked desperate and terrified, and most bizarrely for Peter, he was hysterically crying.

Spider-Man rushed over to untie him.

"It's okay, kid. We're going to get you out of here," he told him.

As he loosened the ropes to free Flash, Spider-Man noticed that the high school student was shaking, almost violently. He was too scared even to stand. Spider-Man steadied Flash as he continued to sob.

"I'm so sorry. It was so stupid of me. So, so stupid!" Flash cried.

"this wasn't your fault,"

Spider-Man said, amazed at himself for feeling bad for Flash.

"But it—it sort of was. There's this kid at school. And he's real scared of you. I thought it was funny, so I . . ."

"You put on a Spider-Man costume to scare him," Spider-Man finished, and Flash nodded.

"You're right, that was stupid," Spider-Man admitted as he whipped away the last rope from Flash's hands. "But not stupid enough to wind up in this position."

"He—he thought I was you," Flash finished. "I was hiding behind the basketball courts and he must have seen me there. He thought I was you and . . ."

Flash began to cry again.

Spider-Man's spider-sense tingled and he turned, expecting the guy he'd webbed up to be behind him. But then he realized that his senses were reacting to something *below*.

He pushed Flash and the chair out of the way and made a fist.

"WELL, IT TOOK YOU LONG ENOUGH, WEBHEAD!" said the Thing from the bottom

of a pit that had to be at least a hundred feet deep. Thing was joined by Daredevil, Nova, and Iron Man.

"This is odd," Spider-Man said.

"Just get us outta here and we'll explain everything," Nova said.

Spider-Man spun a webbed ladder into the pit and slowly the heroes emerged. A few times it looked like the huge Thing might not make it, but he eventually clawed his way up.

Spider-Man told them he'd tied up the guy responsible for this outside.

"LEMME AT 'IM," the Thing said as he stormed out of the shack and the other heroes and Flash followed.

The others explained that the guy who'd captured them called himself the **Chameleon**. He was a master of disguise. He was able to change his skin to look like anyone, or anything. And he could do the same with his clothes, which also responded to his thoughts.

"He could even make clothes that helped him fly?" Spider-Man asked, remembering how **Chameleon** had posed as Nova and Iron Man and flown away.

"Nah, those were some second-rate jet packs," Iron Man said, pointing to the back of the **Chameleon**'s Iron Man suit. The real Iron Man kicked it and it crumbled apart.

"So that's why he couldn't fire a repulsor blast," Spider-Man realized. "And why his Nova blast was so weak."

Spider-Man learned that each of the heroes had been trapped the same way. The **Chameleon** had posed as a fellow hero and led them to the deserted island. Once there he'd told them that there was trouble down an abandoned tunnel, at the other end of the island. Once the heroes were at the far end of the tunnel the **Chameleon** slammed down vibranium walls and trapped the heroes inside, then took on their identities.

"That's why he wanted the **VIBRANIUM** from the museum," Spidey realized. "A little bit of it goes a long way. He could have used even that little chunk of it to reinforce the tunnel."

"He should have thought of that earlier," Nova noted. "The Thing was able to dig through the tunnel floor. I helped burrow through the ground and Daredevil's senses helped us navigate the network of tunnels under this place. We heard the commotion at this end of the island and headed over. That's when you found us."

"JUST TA MAKE SURE, WHY DON'T YA DO SOMETHING TO PROVE YOU ACTUALLY ARE SPIDER-MAN?" the Thing demanded.

"Ta-da,"

Spider-Man said as he landed.

"Who's this guy, then?" Iron Man asked, pointing to Flash.

"Oh, him?"

Spider-Man asked, looking over at Flash. "He's just a kid who's learning that playing games isn't always so much fun."

CHAPTER 10

Led by the Thing, the other heroes took the Chameleon to the authorities, and Flash Thompson back home. Spider-Man raced back to his own home in Queens.

After all, he had homework to finish up.

The next day Midtown High was abuzz with the news. As he

walked down the hall, Peter caught bits of conversation. It was always strange for him to hear some of the things people had to say about Spider-Man's adventures.

By his locker, Peter noticed a group of kids gathered around. As he pushed through the mob, he saw Flash in the middle. He was smiling and laughing and talking to the group.

"Scared? No way, dude, I wasn't scared!" he was saying to a kid standing next to him. "I actually think the Chameleon was scared of *me*! Sure, I played it cool at first, but after he turned off that camera, I got tough. 'Listen,' I said, 'I've got a lot of powerful friends. They'll be looking for me.' And then, of course, Spidey—that's what I call him, 'Spidey'—swooped in to help me out. And together we put the Chameleon away. You know I think Spider-Man is freaking amazing, but even he needs a hand sometimes. I was happy to lend him one."

Peter couldn't help laughing as he walked by, hearing all this. He glanced at Flash and caught his eye. The two of them looked at each other for a second. Then Peter pushed through the rest of the crowd and moved on to his locker.

"I mean, that guy never stood a chance," Flash said. "Between me and Spider-Man—man, he didn't know what he was getting himself into. . . ."

"HEY, PETE!"

Peter turned around to find Gwen. "Crazy what's going on here, huh? I'm just glad Flash is okay. I mean, the guy can be a jerk, but still . . ."

Peter looked at her and smiled.

"Yeah, I guess I know what you mean," he said.

"So, you ready for the test?" Gwen asked, and Peter shrugged, not really sure. He had been studying late into the night.

The morning bell rang. Peter removed his

books and closed his locker. Then he moved through the thinning crowd and walked with Gwen to their first class.

Peter looked back at Flash, who was high-fiving kids as they walked away.

"You'd think he'd learn a thing or two. You know, after being kidnapped by a Super Villain and all," Peter said.

"What makes you so sure he hasn't?" Gwen asked.

"I don't know. I just wouldn't count on it," Peter said, remembering how different the scared and shaking Flash was from the one who was celebrating in the hallway.

As they continued to walk to class, Peter heard someone call his name. Then the person called it again.

"HEY, PARKER!"

Flash shouted out to him from down the hall.

Peter took a deep breath and turned around slowly.

Flash was running toward him. It looked like he had something in his hand. Peter braced himself to block whatever was about to be thrown at him.

"YOU DROPPED THIS OUT OF YOUR LOCKER,"

Flash said, holding out a crumpled piece of paper.

Peter opened it and was surprised and confused by what he saw. He wasn't sure what to say. So he said the natural thing.

"Thanks, Flash."

"Yep, you bet," Flash said. Then he jogged back down the hall to catch up with his friends, who were moving on to whatever they had next on their schedules.

Gwen shot Peter a smile.

"YOU WERE SAYING?"

she asked.

Peter smiled back, happy that for once he wasn't the only one trying to hide a deep, dark secret. And that maybe, just maybe, Spider-Man had helped somebody change. Even if it was just a little bit.

DUFUS
NOT REALLY

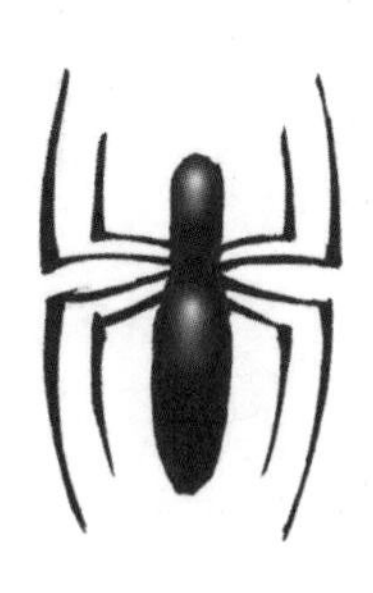